WARNING!

Scaredy Squirrel insists that everyone brush their teeth with germ-fighting toothpaste before reading this book.

For my dentist, Rosa, and for Manuel
Special thanks to Valerie, my friend and publisher,
for seven inspiring years

Published by
Happy Cat Books
An imprint of Catnip Publishing Ltd
14 Greville Street
London EC1N 8SB

First published in paperback 2008
1 3 5 7 9 10 8 6 4 2

First published in Canada by Kids Can Press Ltd, 29 Birch Avenue,
Toronto, ON M4V 1E2

Text and illustrations copyright © 2007 Melanie Watt

The moral right of the author/ illustrator has been asserted

A CIP catalogue record for this book is available from the British Library

ISBN 978-1-905117-65-9

The artwork in this book was rendered in charcoal pencil and acrylic
The text is set in Potato Cut

Printed in China

Scaredy Squirrel

makes a friend

by Melanie Watt

HAPPY CAT BOOKS

Scaredy Squirrel doesn't have a friend.
He'd rather be alone than risk encountering
someone dangerous. A squirrel could get bitten.

A few individuals
Scaredy Squirrel
is afraid to be
bitten by:

walruses

bunnies

beavers

piranhas

Godzilla

So Scaredy Squirrel
finds interesting ways
to pass the time all
by himself.

He reads.

He whistles.

He crafts.

He yawns.

He knits.

He chats.

He counts.

Until one day he spots . . .

goldfish

Someone
perfectly safe!

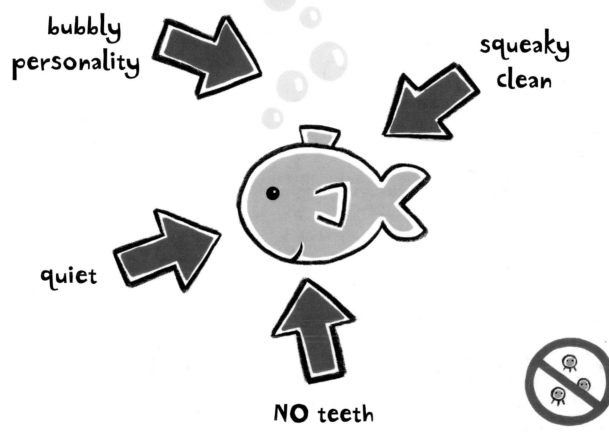

A few items Scaredy Squirrel needs to make the Perfect Friend:

lemon	name tag	mittens	comb

mirror	air freshener	toothbrush	chew toy

HELLO
my name is

The Perfect Plan

Step 1: Toss down chew toy to distract biters

Step 2: Use mirror to check hair and teeth

Step 3: Run to fountain

Step 4: Point to name tag and smile

Step 5: Offer lemonade

Step 6: Make the Perfect Friend

Legend

	nut tree
	fountain
	tree
	rocks
	bush
	pine tree
	pond
	biter
	biter
	biter
	biter
	biter

I am here.

Don't talk to suspicious bunnies.

Stay away from piranha-infested ponds.

Beware of walruses: they're fast on their flippers.

Goldfish is here.

Avoid beavers: they could snap at any moment.

Watch out for Godzilla — for obvious reasons!

BUT let's say, just for example, that Scaredy Squirrel **DID** come face to face with a potential biter. He knows exactly what **NOT** to do ...

 **DO NOT** show fear.

 **DO NOT** show your fingers.

 **DO NOT** make eye contact.

 **DO NOT** make any loud noises.

 If all else fails, **PLAY DEAD** . . .

And hand over the Test.

Scaredy's Risk Test

1) Who are you?

☐ (walrus) ☐ (pufferfish)

☐ (rabbit) ☐ (dinosaur)

☐ (beaver) other ☐

2) How many teeth do you have?

2 ☐   100 ☐

10 ☐   1000 ☐

32 ☐   more ☐

3) What's your hobby?

biting ☐

other ☐

4) What do you see?

friend ☐   something ☐
              to bite

objects in mirror are closer than they appear

And he realizes . . .

The dog chases Scaredy around the bush . . .

around the fountain . . .

Time out!

and around in circles . . .

until Scaredy Squirrel . . .

Plays DEAD.

30 minutes later

1 hour later

2 hours later

After all this time, Scaredy Squirrel realizes that the dog doesn't want to bite him ...

He just wants a friend!

Scaredy Squirrel points to his name tag and smiles.

Then he starts chasing his new buddy.

They play fetch.

They play hide-and-seek.

And they play dead.

Scaredy Squirrel forgets all about the goldfish, not to mention the walruses, bunnies, beavers, piranhas and Godzilla.

Time flies when you're having fun!

All this excitement inspires Scaredy Squirrel to make a few minor changes to his idea of a friend . . .

P.S. As for the
wet doggy smell,
it's been taken care of.